The Phantom of Shrieking Pond

Suzanne Weyn

PRICE STERN SLOAN
Los Angeles

For Carolan Suzanne Weyn
with love

Published by Price Stern Sloan, Inc.
11150 Olympic Boulevard
Los Angeles, California 90064
ISBN: 0-8431-3411-9
Printed in the United States of America
10 9 8 7 6 5 4 3 2

Contents

A Warning

"What happened to our beautiful spring day?" Barbie wondered aloud.

"It's disappeared," said Ken, sitting in the passenger seat of Barbie's red convertible and glancing up at the sky. "Maybe we should put the top on."

Barbie pulled to the side of the road. At the start of this trip, the sky had been a brilliant blue. But as they drove, black storm clouds had gathered.

A car pulled off the road and parked behind them. "Everything OK?" asked Midge, sticking her head out the car window.

While Ken took the top from the trunk, Barbie walked over to her best friend. Beside Midge was Midge's husband, Alan. In the backseat sat Barbie's good friend Kira and Barbie's younger sister, Skipper. "Ken is just putting on the top," Barbie explained.

"We're almost there," said Midge.

"Are you excited?" asked Barbie.

"Excited is not the word!" exclaimed Midge. "I can't believe Aunt Sara left me that big old house in her will. It's been a while since I last saw it. When Aunt Sara moved to Florida two years ago, she just boarded up the place."

"We'd better get going," said Alan. "Maybe we can stay ahead of this storm."

"Let me pull out first, and you can follow," said Midge to Barbie. "I'll have to stop for gas."

"OK. See you at the first gas station," said Barbie.

They had put the top on just in time. As soon as Barbie got back on the road, big raindrops plopped onto her windshield. "I sure hope the house is in decent shape," said Barbie, clicking on her wipers. "It would be so wonderful if Midge could really turn it into a camp for children."

"It was nice of you to suggest we all come with her," said Ken. "If the place is in bad shape, she'll need a lot of help. Old, empty houses tend to fall apart after a while. Mice and bugs also have a way of moving in."

Barbie wrinkled her nose. "Mice and bugs? Yuck!" Then she smiled. "Well, what breaks can be fixed. And creatures that move in can be moved out."

"That's typical can-do Barbie thinking," Ken said with a grin.

Lightning cracked open the dark sky as they drove into the small town of Chillborn. Rain fell in a sheet, and thunder boomed directly above them.

Barbie followed Midge's car into a small gas station.

Midge ran over to Barbie's car. "They sell snacks inside," she said. "Want anything?"

"I'll come with you," Barbie said.

Midge and Barbie ran into the service station

and took cold sodas from the refrigerator case. They put the items on the counter.

"Some storm, eh?" said the teenage boy behind the counter. "Where you headed?"

"To the old Jacob house," Midge replied.

The boy went pale. "The mansion?"

Midge laughed. "I guess it is pretty big. I'm not sure it's a mansion, though."

"It is," the boy insisted seriously. "It's a haunted mansion."

"Haunted?" asked Barbie.

"Sure," said the boy. "We call it the Haunted Mansion at Shrieking Pond."

"What?" Midge scoffed. "There's a pond by the house, but I never heard it shriek."

"It shrieks all right," said the boy. "And last summer some kids saw a phantom there!"

"I don't believe that," said Barbie.

"All five of them saw it. And they're not the only ones. Other people have seen the Phantom of Shrieking Pond."

"Gee, Midge," said Barbie. "It looks like

you've inherited your very own phantom."

"Don't laugh," warned the boy. "I'd turn right around if I were you."

"Thanks for the warning," Midge said lightly.

Outside, Barbie and Midge stood for a moment under the overhanging roof. "That's all nonsense, don't you think?" said Midge.

"Of course it is," agreed Barbie.

They got back into their cars. Barbie followed Midge along more roads. Finally they turned up a long, muddy drive. At the end stood the old Jacob house.

"Did you see that?" Barbie asked suddenly. As she peered through her rain-soaked windshield, she thought she saw a light. The moment she spotted it, it had snapped off.

"Are you talking about that light?" asked Ken.

Barbie nodded. "Could someone be in there?"

"I doubt it," said Ken. "Maybe it was the glare from our headlights."

As he spoke, a bright flash of lightning lit the

house from behind. Its porch jutted out eerily. Black boarded-up windows seemed to peer at them like hollow eyes.

"I don't believe in haunted houses," said Ken. "But if I did, this would sure look like one."

2

The Phantom in the Closet

"Oh, this is a disaster!" groaned Midge.

Barbie shined her flashlight down the hall. Though it was only late afternoon, the stormy sky and boarded windows made the house pitch-dark. But even by flashlight, it was easy to see what Midge meant.

The house was a shambles. Large patches of plaster hung from the ceiling. The wallpaper was peeling, and the floors were cracked.

"We can't afford to fix up this place," Midge cried. "I can just forget the whole idea of having a camp."

"Stay calm," said Ken. "If we had some light, we could get a better look at this. The electricity isn't on, is it?"

"I don't think so," Midge replied.

"I thought I saw a light as we drove up, but then it went out," said Barbie.

"You're scaring me!" Skipper said, only half joking.

Ken laughed. "I know how we can solve this mystery," he said. "We just have to find the fuse box."

Barbie and Ken searched the dark house. "There it is," said Ken. They crossed to a dusty metal box on the wall. "All the fuses are out," he observed.

"Which means I couldn't have seen a light," said Barbie.

"But I saw it too. Like I said, it was probably just a reflection," said Ken.

"But Ken, the windows are boarded. They wouldn't throw a reflection."

Ken looked at her. "You're right, but then we wouldn't have seen a light either."

"This is very strange," said Barbie.

When they got back upstairs, the house was

aglow with warm light. Kira was lighting one of several candles attached to the wall. The light threw long shadows around the room.

"At least now we can see," said Barbie.

"Yeah. We can see how awful the place really is," muttered Midge.

Just then there was a loud rapping on the front door. Midge's hand flew to her mouth in fright. "Who could that be?"

"It was a dark and stormy night," Kira teased. "A loud rapping was heard at the door. Icy fingers of fear ran up their spines as the door flew open." Dramatically, Kira flung open the front door.

"Hi, guys!" said Christie, shaking her drenched raincoat.

Her boyfriend, Steve, was at her side. "This is some storm," he said, stepping inside.

Midge laughed. "I guess I'm a little edgy," she admitted.

"Who wouldn't be? Look at this place," said

Christie. "Sorry we're so late. We got a late start, and the driving was horrible."

"That's OK," said Midge. "You haven't missed much. The place is falling apart. A kid told me it's haunted, and there's no light."

"Well, I always say there's nothing like a good challenge," said Christie. "By the way, where is the old Skipper-roo?"

"She's off exploring," said Alan.

"That's Skipper." Christie said. "Always looking for something to—"

Suddenly a piercing scream came from the second floor. "Skipper!" cried Barbie, racing up the stairs.

"Barbie!" Skipper screamed. Barbie followed Skipper's panicked voice down a long hallway. The rest of the gang was behind her.

"Skipper, what's wrong?" Barbie gasped as she ran into a large bedroom.

With a quivering hand, Skipper pointed to the closet. "There's something in there!"

"Oh, Skipper," Barbie said, laughing gently. "You're letting your imagination run away with—" Barbie cut herself short. She'd heard a sound. There <u>was</u> something in the closet.

There was a long, mournful moan.

"What is it?" asked Midge, reaching the doorway ahead of the others.

"There's a ghost—or something—in that closet," Skipper reported.

"Don't open it," said Midge, backing up.

The rest of the gang appeared.

"Did I hear some silliness about a ghost?" asked Christie.

Another moan came from inside the closet. We—aaaaaaaa—aaaaaaa!

"I'm going to open that door!" said Barbie.

She yanked the doorknob. At first she saw only an empty closet. Then she looked down.

"Kittens!" she cried.

3

Shrieking Pond

"I found this on the porch," said Kira, holding a basket. "I'll cushion it with my sweatshirt."

Midge, Christie and Barbie knelt near the open door of the closet where the mother cat and her five squirming, newborn kittens lay.

Kira bent to pick up a tiny kitten. "I'm getting my camera and taking some pictures of these guys."

The mother cat hissed at Kira. "Okay, Mama," Kira said, laughing. "You can have him back."

"I feel silly," said Skipper, sitting on the bed. "I pushed that door shut when I came in. I guess I locked the cat in."

"Don't feel bad," said Midge. "I thought there was a ghost in there too."

Alan, Ken and Steve had gone exploring, but now they appeared in the doorway. "We've been looking around the place," said Steve. "It doesn't look too bad."

Midge sighed. "I hope you're right," she said.

"Listen!" said Christie. "The rain has stopped."

"Want to take a walk?" Ken asked Barbie.

"Sure," she replied.

Downstairs, Barbie pulled on her jean jacket and stepped out onto the porch with Ken. "Do you really think there might be some hope for this place?" she asked him.

"We'll know tomorrow when we have some good light," he replied. "It all depends on whether the plumbing, the furnace, the electric wiring and the roof are all right. Those things cost the most to fix."

"I'll keep my fingers crossed," Barbie said. "This place could be a great camp."

"As long as it's not haunted," Ken said.

"Ken, you don't really think that could be true, do you?" asked Barbie, surprised.

"Anything is possible," he teased in a ghostly voice.

"I don't scare so easily," Barbie said, laughing. She looked out at the grounds and breathed the moist air. "I bet it will be beautiful tomorrow, and this place will look much better," she said.

"Let's look around," Ken said.

As they walked through the long, rain-drenched grass, Barbie glanced up at the boarded windows on the top floor. "Look, Ken," she said. "The sunset is gleaming off that window way at the top. It looks like it's boarded from the inside, instead of the outside."

"Then it _was_ a reflection we saw," Ken said.

"I wonder why it's boarded differently," Barbie said.

They headed on along the misty, softly

rolling hills. Lilac trees clustered around the pond. "Smell those lilacs!" cried Barbie. "I'm going to bring some of these flowers inside. That will cheer Midge up."

"This must be the terrifying Shrieking Pond," Ken said with a smile.

Barbie began snapping off low-hanging lilac blooms. "Isn't that silly!" she exclaimed. "But you know, I think that boy got to Midge. She's always been like that."

Barbie continued picking lilacs. After a few minutes, she heard something strange—a low, warbling sound. And it was growing louder. She looked at Ken. From his expression, she could tell he was listening too. "What do you think that is?" she asked, puzzled.

"Maybe it's some kind of bird," he suggested.

Holding her lilacs, Barbie went to Ken's side. "If so, it's the strangest bird I've ever heard. It sounds so creepy."

Suddenly Barbie dropped her flowers. "Ken!"

she gasped. "Over there!"

At the far end of the pond stood a shimmering white phantom. Fog rose up around its form. With a terrifying shriek, it raised its arms. Then it wailed as if it was crying out to the heavens above.

Barbie grabbed Ken's arm. "That can't be real. Let's catch whoever it is," she said, breaking into a run.

4

The Haunting

"I don't believe this!" cried Barbie breathlessly. She stood at the bottom of a grassy hill, looking around. Ken was just behind her. "It disappeared," she told him. "Vanished into thin air like…like…"

"Like a phantom?" said Ken.

Barbie nodded. "If I didn't know better, I'd have to say yes…like a phantom." The moment Barbie and Ken began running, the ghostly figure had fled. Barbie had almost caught up with it when the figure leaped down over the side of a hill and disappeared.

"Did it look like a man or a woman to you?" Ken asked.

"It was hard to tell. I think it was a woman, though," Barbie answered."Let's see if anyone else saw it," Ken suggested.

Barbie agreed. But no sooner did they step into the dark house than they heard Midge cry out from the second floor.

Barbie and Ken bounded up the stairs and found Midge standing in the hallway. "What is it?" asked Barbie, putting her arm around her friend.

"Look in there," said Midge, her voice full of fear. "Look in that room!"

Barbie and Ken hurried into the room. "Oh, my gosh," Barbie said quietly. "What happened?" The mattress had been tossed off the bed. Midge and Alan's suitcases lay open on the floor. Their clothing had been thrown all around. The four drawers of the one dresser had been pulled out and lay at odd angles around the bedroom.

"I came in and put down our suitcases," said Midge from the doorway. "This room had some dust and cobwebs, but it didn't look anything like this!"

Barbie and Ken exchanged glances. Could this be the work of the phantom?

Midge studied them. "You guys aren't telling me something. What is it?" she demanded.

Just then, Kira appeared in the doorway. "Have any of you seen the kittens?" she asked. "They're not in the closet."

"Maybe the mother cat took them somewhere private," Barbie suggested.

"I don't think she could have taken the basket, too," said Kira.

Kira glanced around the room. "What happened?"

"I wish I knew," said Midge. "That kid in town wasn't fooling. I'm for getting out of here right now."

"There has to be an explanation for all this," Barbie said sensibly. "I say we all get together and figure out what's going on."

Barbie went through the house and rounded up the gang. They gathered on the first floor. It was now getting very dark. Only their flashlights and the flickering flames from the wall candles lit the room.

No one had seen the cat, and no one had been near Midge and Alan's room. Barbie told them about the strange figure near the pond and how it had vanished.

"You saw the Phantom of Shrieking Pond!" Skipper cried. "That's who's doing this."

"I'm sorry I dragged you all up here," Midge apologized. "There's a hotel in town. I bet it has some vacant rooms."

"Don't be silly," said Christie. She looked at Steve and narrowed her eyes. "Steve, if this is your idea of a joke, I'll—"

"Hey, I'm innocent!" Steve protested. "Besides, Alan and I have taken some of the boards off the windows. The place won't look so bleak tomorrow."

"But how do you explain what happened to my room?" asked Midge. "And where are the cats? Not to mention that...that...thing you saw out by the pond."

"I don't know," Barbie admitted. "But I don't think we should run just because we're spooked. It's been a long day. Let's go to sleep early."

The gang went upstairs to the second floor. "I'm not sleeping in that room where our stuff was tossed around," Midge said firmly. "How about all of us throwing our sleeping bags down in the big bedroom."

"Sounds good to me," agreed Kira.

The gang laid out their sleeping bags.

"I'm glad the guys took the boards off this window," said Skipper, snuggling into her sleeping bag. "It's less creepy."

"Once the place is fixed up, it won't seem creepy at all," Barbie said. "You'll see."

Barbie fell asleep quickly. She had been sleeping for several hours when something woke her. It was a light hovering just inside the window. Sitting up, Barbie rubbed her eyes. Then she sucked in her breath sharply. It was more than a light. It was a glowing face! And it was floating in the air before her!

5

Barbie's Discovery

I'm getting to the bottom of all this, thought Barbie. She sat up, clutching her flashlight. The moment she had shined it on the floating head, it had disappeared!

Silently, Barbie got out of her sleeping bag. She pulled a sweater over her nightshirt and stepped into the dark hall.

At the end of the hall was a stairway to the third floor. Midge had wanted everyone to wait for daylight to go up there. Barbie decided not to wait.

With her flashlight shining, she carefully climbed the creaky stairs. Nobody, not even a ghost, is going to keep those kids from getting their camp, she thought, determined.

Barbie didn't believe in ghosts. But even if she was wrong—even if this house <u>was</u>

haunted—she wasn't giving up. It's just like with the mice, she told herself. Unwelcome guests can always be moved out.

Barbie didn't know <u>how</u> ghosts could be forced to leave, but she wasn't going to be frightened off.

When she reached the third floor, Barbie swept her flashlight beam along the walls. Portraits in gold frames hung here and there. They were very old-fashioned. One portrait was a woman who looked a lot like Midge.

All the women pictured wore beautiful jewels. Sometimes different people wore the same pieces of jewelry. The pieces must have been passed on from mother to daughter, Barbie figured.

Gently, Barbie pushed open the doors she passed. All the rooms were empty.

She wasn't exactly sure what she was looking for. The phantom? A person? The cats?

She needed to find something that would

give her a clue to what was going on.

At the end of the hallway, she noticed a square wood hatch in the ceiling. A pull-cord hung from it, dangling high above her head.

Barbie jumped, but she couldn't reach the cord. Then she noticed a chair in the corner. She positioned it under the hatch door. The chair wobbled when she stood on it, but she was able to reach the cord.

One good yank and the hatch door swung down out of the ceiling. Attached to the inside of the door was a foldout ladder. It fell open in front of her.

Brave as she was, Barbie shivered at the thought of climbing that ladder. She might not find the phantom—but there was a good chance she'd find mice, rats or even bats!

She sucked in her breath and began to climb. Soon she could see into the attic. She had been prepared to find many things. But not what she saw by the beam of her flashlight.

The room was furnished with antiques. A ruffled spread covered the four-poster bed. Lace pillows were laid at the head of the bed, and a quilt was folded neatly at the foot.

In a corner near the only window was a table and one chair. Barbie noticed that the window wasn't boarded. Indoor shutters merely gave the impression that it was.

Barbie climbed up into the room and walked over to the table. On it was a large lamp and a box of matches. She was surprised to see that there was no sign of dust—as if someone had recently cleaned.

Barbie lit the lamp. The room was filled with light. This is the light I saw when we drove up, she realized.

Suddenly, something behind the bed moved. Barbie jumped back. She waited, her heart pounding wildly.

The cat leapt onto the bed. Barbie sighed with relief. She went over to the cat and scratched it behind its ears. On the floor were the kittens, nestled in the basket.

Barbie glanced around the room. Was someone living here? It was hard to tell. There was no refrigerator, no TV, no closet, no food—not even for the cats. It wasn't set up for a person to live in.

But it would be a perfect room for the phantom, Barbie thought. For a moment, her imagination took over. She pictured that glowing head appearing again. And now she would be trapped with it, in this strange room.

"Stop!" she scolded herself out loud. She decided to wake the others and see what they thought. She began to climb down—then froze on the ladder. She had heard something on the floor below. It had sounded like someone running!

6

A Race into Darkness

Barbie dropped quickly to the floor and begun chasing after the person making the footsteps.

Only there was no person. The hall was empty.

But the footsteps had been loud, as if the person was very close.

Barbie felt her no-such-thing-as-ghosts attitude fading. There <u>had</u> been footsteps in the hall. Yet no one was here.

Barbie hurried back to the second floor. She was just at the bottom of the stairs when someone turned the hall corner.

"Ah!" Barbie gasped. The person facing her leapt back. "Oh, you scared me!" Midge panted, her hand over her heart.

"Why are you up?" Barbie asked.

"I heard someone walking around on the third floor," Midge explained. "I guess it was you."

"Maybe it wasn't," said Barbie. "I heard footsteps too. Only I didn't see anyone."

Midge grabbed Barbie's wrist. "That does it," she said as she began pulling Barbie down the hall. "We're getting out of here right now."

Barbie dug in her heels. "Wait. I want you to see something I found in the attic. It's a room—the room where we saw the light. The cats are up there."

"The cats?" Midge stared at Barbie. "You mean someone is living upstairs?"

"Well, yes...but it's hard to tell."

"What do you mean?" Midge asked.

"Come upstairs and I'll show you."

Midge frowned. "I don't want to, but now you've got me curious. I visited here a lot when I was a kid. Aunt Sara never let us go up into the attic. She said it was too dangerous. Gee, I wonder if Aunt Sara knew there was something creepy about that attic room even back then."

"Come on," said Barbie. She and Midge headed up the stairs. As soon as they stepped onto the third floor, Barbie knew something was wrong. She had left the lamp lit and the hatch door open. There should have been a light at the end of the hall. But there wasn't.

Barbie ran to the hatch with Midge close behind. "Someone shut it!" she cried.

"Or some<u>thing</u>," added Midge.

The chair stood under the hatch where Barbie had left it. She climbed up and yanked at the cord. The hatch wouldn't budge!

"This is so strange," Barbie told Midge. "It opened easily the last time."

Barbie climbed down from the chair. "Someone must have locked it from in—"

Barbie cut herself short and clutched Midge's arm. "Listen! Do you hear it?"

The sound was unmistakable. There were definitely footsteps coming from somewhere. But this time they weren't running. They walked slowly back and forth.

"It sounds like the steps are right here in the hall with us," Midge observed, her voice quivering.

Barbie forced herself to stay calm. "But Midge, there's a rug on this floor," she pointed out. "Footsteps wouldn't make that kind of clattering sound on this rug."

"OK," said Midge. "Then where are they coming from?"

Barbie listened hard. <u>Click-clack</u>, <u>click-clack</u>. There was a pause, and then more steps.

Barbie's eyes widened. "Midge! The sound is coming from inside this wall!"

"That proves it's a ghost, don't you think?" said Midge, going pale.

Barbie ran her hands along the wall where she'd heard the sound. "It could mean something else," she said.

"What else could it mean?" asked Midge. "And what are you doing?"

Before Barbie could answer, a section of the wall swung open in front of them. "It could mean there are hidden tunnels in this house," Barbie said, gazing into the dark passageway.

"How did you do that?" Midge gasped.

"I found a small switch under the frame of this painting," Barbie explained. "It was just a hunch."

Barbie shined her light inside. The walls were plain wood. Old planks were nailed together to make a floor. Again, the footsteps sounded. Barbie snapped off her light. "The phantom is coming toward us," she whispered to Midge.

The steps came closer and closer. They were coming from the direction of the attic. In the darkness, Barbie couldn't see a thing. Then the steps stopped abruptly. It was as if whoever was approaching had sensed that

Barbie and Midge were waiting at the passage entrance.

"Let's go," said Barbie. She and Midge ran into the passage. The quickness of the steps ahead of them told Barbie that the person—or phantom—was fleeing. They kept running. The steps got louder. They were closing the distance between them.

All of a sudden she heard a crash behind her, followed by a scream! Barbie whirled around and shined her light behind her. Midge had disappeared!

7

No Way Out!

"Get me out of here!" cried Midge, looking up at Barbie from below the floor. Midge had tripped and fallen. She'd stepped on a rotten floorboard that had given in. Now she was in a space just tall enough for her to stand.

"Are you hurt?" Barbie asked.

"Not much. I just banged my knee on something hard. It's bleeding."

Barbie aimed her light around the floor near Midge. "You must have hit that metal box by your foot," she guessed.

"Ow, my knee!" Midge winced as she bent to look at the box. Barbie trained her light on it while Midge pried it open.

"Oh!" they gasped at once. Brilliant, glittering jewelry shone up at them. Midge handed the box up to Barbie. She set it aside, then reached her arm into the hole. "Come on, Midge. I'll pull you up."

It took all Barbie's strength to pull Midge from the hole, but finally she was out. "We've lost our ghost," Barbie said. "I don't hear any more footsteps."

"Let's just get out of here," said Midge, holding her knee. "We can check out these jewels later."

"You're right," Barbie agreed. Picking up the box of jewels, she headed toward the tunnel entrance with Midge behind her. After a few moments, she stopped. "I think we've passed the opening," she said.

"Which means the opening is no longer open," Midge pointed out grimly.

"Once we find it, we can probably push it open or find another lever," Barbie said hopefully. They walked back, feeling along the wall. "Here it is," said Barbie. "I can feel the hinges." She and Midge threw their weight against the wall. It didn't move.

Barbie swept her light all along the wall, but she didn't see a latch or a switch. She shined the light behind her. Up ahead, in the opposite direction of the attic, the tunnel continued. "Maybe there is another way out," she said.

As she spoke, her light dimmed and then flickered. Midge moaned. "Please don't tell me your batteries are running out," she said.

"They do seem low," Barbie replied.

Midge began stomping on the floor with her good leg. "Help!" she cried. "Somebody wake up!"

"Don't bother," Barbie said. "We'll have to find another way to get their attention."

"I guess you're right," Midge agreed glumly. "I wonder why there are two floors, anyway."

"It probably has something to do with the way they built these secret passages," Barbie said. "Don't worry. This passage has to come out somewhere. Our ghost went toward the attic, so let's try going the other way."

"Absolutely," said Midge. "I'm all for walking <u>away</u> from the ghost, not toward it." Just then Barbie's flashlight flickered one last time and went out, plunging them into darkness. "Great!" said Midge. "I can't even see you. You <u>are</u> still there, aren't you?"

"Yes. I'm right here," Barbie answered, touching Midge's shoulder. "If we keep moving along the wall, we should be OK." I hope, she added silently.

They had been groping their way through the darkness for several minutes when Barbie put her foot out and almost stepped off into thin air. "Oh, my gosh!" she cried, catching her balance at the last moment. "The floor ends here. Maybe there are stairs."

Sure enough, when she stuck her foot down, she hit a wooden rung. "Can your bad knee handle a ladder?" she asked Midge.

"I'll have to try," Midge said gamely.

"I'll go first," Barbie said. "You take it slow." With the box in one hand, Barbie began climbing down the ladder. Soon she came to a door beside the ladder. She tried it, but it was locked. "This must be another passage on the second floor, but we can't get to it," she shouted up to Midge. "We'll have to keep climbing down."

They passed another locked door. Barbie guessed it led to the ground floor. Yet the ladder kept going down. Maybe there's an open door in the basement, Barbie thought.

After more climbing, they came to another door. With a quick turn of the knob, it creaked open.

Barbie stepped through the door onto a dirt floor. "Now where the heck does this lead?" asked Midge.

"This must be the basement," said Barbie.

Feeling along the icy wall, they continued

through the tunnel. "It's freezing down here!" Midge exclaimed.

"I wonder if this tunnel is taking us outside," Barbie replied. "If we're underground, that explains why it's so cold."

"I don't like this," said Midge. "What if we never get out of here? Then we'll be the Phantoms of Shrieking Pond. Oh, gosh, maybe this is what happened to the phantom who is haunting this place!"

"Midge, look!" cried Barbie. Farther down the tunnel, about twenty yards away, was a streak of gentle sunlight!

8

The Phantom Appears

Barbie pulled herself up onto the dewy grass. She couldn't believe it was already dawn.

Beside her was the metal box she'd tossed up onto the ground from below and the door she'd just pushed up and over. Lying on her stomach, she helped pull Midge out of the tunnel.

It turned out that the tunnel leading from the basement wasn't far below ground. Once they found the opening, it was easy to climb up.

"Dawn never looked so good," said Midge, sitting beside Barbie. As she spoke, Midge opened the box of jewels. She whistled softly. "Would you look at these!"

Barbie gazed at the jewels thoughtfully. "I've seen some of these pieces before," she said, trying to recall where. She lifted a necklace from the box. "I know!" she cried. "The portraits on the third floor! There's a woman in one of them who looks just like you. She's wearing this."

"That's Aunt Margaret," said Midge. "And you're right. She is wearing this necklace."

"A lot of this jewelry is in those paintings," said Barbie, sorting through the glittering gems. "These must have been passed down through your family for years."

"I wonder why they were hidden in the floor," said Midge. "I can't wait to get back to the house and compare these to the jewelry in the portraits."

"I can't wait to go back and check out this tunnel," said Barbie. "It keeps going, past where we came up. I want to see that attic room again too."

Barbie got to her feet. They had come out at the bottom of a steep hill. "Midge, this is the exact spot where the ghost disappeared yesterday! Don't you know what that means?"

"That the so-called ghost really slipped down this tunnel," Midge said.

Barbie nodded. "Let's get back to the house. We have a lot of exploring to do today. We'll need the gang to help us."

When they reached the house, it was quiet. Midge laughed. "They don't even realize we were gone," she said.

Just then they heard Alan shouting from upstairs. "Midge! Barbie! Where are you?"

"They know now," Barbie said, smiling. "We're down here!" she called out.

Alan and Skipper ran halfway down the stairs. Ken, Kira, Christie and Steve were right behind them. "I guess we're all a little nervous," Alan said, laughing.

"That's all right," said Midge. "We almost <u>did</u> need you to search for us."

"What do you mean?" Alan asked.

"It's a strange story," said Barbie. "You'd better all come down and hear it."

Yawning and half-awake, the gang gathered around the large dining room table. Barbie and Midge began telling them everything that had happened.

"You must have been scared to death!" said Christie.

"Let's see the jewels," Skipper said, opening the box.

"There's a fortune here!" said Ken.

A sudden noise in the corner of the room caused everyone to turn at once. It sounded as if someone had gasped sharply.

"There's a crack in that panel," said Kira. "Maybe it opens to another secret passage."

Barbie ran to the corner of the room and stuck her fingers into the crack. Instantly the panel gave way. In the passage, footsteps clattered away.

This time Barbie was determined not to let the phantom escape. She sprinted down the low passage. The gang was right behind her. It wasn't long before she gained on the small, bent figure fleeing from her. She couldn't yet tell if it was a man or a woman, but it was definitely not a ghost!

Barbie reached out and grabbed the person's bony shoulder. It was an old woman! "Don't hurt me! Please!" she cried, cringing in fear.

"No one will hurt you," said Barbie, "But we do need some answers."

In a moment, her friends caught up to Barbie. Hobbling on her hurt leg, Midge was the last to arrive.

"Here's the phantom, Midge," said Steve.

Midge's jaw dropped. "Amy!" she cried. "What are you doing here?"

9

Amy's Story

The old woman sat up straight in a dining room chair. Her wiry white hair was cut short, and her face was deeply lined. "I didn't realize it was you, Midge, dear," she said. "You've changed so since you were a child."

"Amy used to be Aunt Sara's personal secretary," Midge explained to the group. "She was with her for more than fifteen years, until Aunt Sara moved to Florida."

"Now that the jewels are found, I may join her in Florida," said Amy.

"Aunt Sara died three months ago," Midge told her gently.

The old woman's eyes welled with tears. "Now she'll never know the truth," she said. "It's all been for nothing."

"Amy, you'd better start at the beginning,"

said Barbie. "Are you the Phantom of Shrieking Pond?"

Amy nodded. "I'm afraid so. It was the only way I could think of to keep the local kids from coming up here and making a mess."

"But why are you <u>here</u>?" Kira asked.

"Because of the jewels," Amy said. "Sara accused me of stealing them."

"Did you steal them?" asked Christie.

"Absolutely not," said Amy. "They were misplaced by Midge's Uncle Willis, God rest his soul. Before he died, his mind began slipping. Sara didn't want to see it, but it was true. He gathered the jewels—which were the family fortune—and hid them. He said bankers were all thieves and couldn't be trusted. Then the poor soul forgot he'd done it. All he knew was that the jewels were gone."

"Why did they think you took them?" Barbie asked.

"I was the only other person in the house. They had no choice but to believe I'd taken them. Sara felt so betrayed. It's one of the reasons she left the house and never came back."

"I still don't understand what you're doing here," Ken said.

"I was trying to clear my name," said Amy. "My dream was to find the jewels and then present them to Sara. She was my dearest friend. I hated that we parted on such bad terms."

"You've been looking for the jewels for two years?" asked Steve.

"Yes," said Amy. "Every day I would search another part of the house or the grounds. In the past two years, I've covered every inch of this place." Amy laughed bitterly. "Every inch but the one you young ladies discovered last night."

"But your room," Barbie questioned, "there's no food or clothing in it."

"That's not where I really live. If you had followed that tunnel past where you climbed out, you would have come to my house. It's a small cottage. It used to belong to the grounds keeper. But I'm old, and it's a long walk back and forth between this house and my cottage. I keep that room in the attic as a resting place. And it's haunting headquarters when there are kids in the house."

"I never knew about these secret passages," said Midge. "Why didn't Aunt Sara ever mention it?"

"She didn't want you kids to get trapped in the passages or hurt on those old floorboards," Amy replied. "This house used to be part of the Underground Railroad that helped runaway slaves escape to Canada. They'd come into the cottage, take the tunnel into the house and stay in the attic room until they were rested and ready to go on."

"When I saw you young people, I thought Sara had sold the house," Amy said. "I couldn't take a chance of having to leave before I found those jewels. I hoped I could scare you out. I guess you folks don't scare so easily."

"Some of us don't," said Midge, smiling at Barbie.

"How did you make that face appear at my window?" Barbie asked.

"The face was just an image from a slide machine. I projected it through a small hole in the wall from the next room."

"But there's no electricity in this house," said Ken. "How could you have used the projector?"

"It runs on a battery pack," Amy replied.

"What will you do now?" Midge asked.

Amy shook her head sadly. "I don't know. I've been in this house for twenty years. But I'll pack up and be out of here by night. Sorry for all the worry I caused you. I wouldn't have hurt anyone. I didn't even know you girls were shut up in the passage. That old door has a way of slowly closing all by itself."

Her head bent, Amy got up to leave.

"Wait," Barbie said. "I might have an idea that could work for everyone."

10

A Great Idea

Midge and Barbie stood in the hall, talking softly. "Do you trust her enough?" Barbie asked. "You'll have to if my plan is going to work."

Midge gave the question a moment's thought. "Yes, I do," she said. "She's always been spunky and determined. What she's done here is a bit odd, but it shows that she's loyal and isn't easily discouraged."

Barbie smiled. "That's for sure."

"Barbie, you're a genius," said Midge. "Let's go tell Amy your idea."

Barbie and Midge returned to the dining room. Everyone was waiting for them. "Here's the deal," said Midge to Amy. "Selling these jewels will certainly give me enough money to fix up this place. So it's full steam ahead on project Kids' Camp!"

The gang cheered. Even Amy smiled. "I couldn't think of a better use for this house," she said.

"I'm glad you think so," Midge continued, "because I'd like you to stay on here. You could be in charge of keeping up the house in the winter, and be camp administrator during the summer. I remember how organized you are. I think you'd be perfect. What do you say?"

Joyful tears sprang to the old woman's eyes. "I say it's too good to believe. I love this place, but it's been a lonely life. Now to see it full of happy, laughing children again..." She buried her face in her hands and wept with emotion.

Barbie put her arm around the woman. "I think you'll do a great job," she said.

"I hope you can stand the sound of hammering, though," said Ken. "You'll be hearing a lot of it."

"That's all right," said Amy. "Nothing would delight me more than to see this place come back to life."

"Like a phantom?" asked Skipper with a twinkle in her eye.

Midge laughed. "Don't even say that word! I never want to hear it again."

"This place does need a ton of work," said Barbie. "And there's no time like now to get started."

Midge sighed happily. "I can just see it. I'm going to fill this house with bright, happy colors."

The gang lost no time. Alan and Ken went up to the roof and began replacing fallen tiles. Kira and Steve worked on the plumbing leaks.

Midge, Barbie, Christie and Skipper went into the old living room. White sheets covered the furniture. They left them on while they scraped the walls. Then they painted the room a lively cornflower blue.

While the paint dried, they took a trip into town. They returned with pretty throw pillows, flowered drapes and yellow and blue scatter rugs.

"I have an idea," said Christie as she dusted the fireplace mantel. "I wouldn't mind coming up as a counselor. I could teach the kids to use Rollerblade® in-line skates. I've been learning to do it myself."

"You can count on me, too," Barbie said as she pulled a sheet off a chair.

"I've always wanted to be a junior counselor," Skipper chimed in.

"You guys are the best," said Midge. "I don't think I can get this place ready until August. It will be hard work."

Christie laughed. "That never bothers us," she said.

"But you know what?" said Barbie. "Since we'll be busy in August, we should have some summer fun in July."

"Do you have a plan?" asked Christie.

Barbie smiled. "As a matter of fact, I do. A cousin of mine just built a hotel by the ocean in California. He asked me and my friends to come and stay anytime we wanted. It's a big place."

"That sounds fabulous!" cried Christie. "I can just see me skating down the boardwalk now."

"I'll bring my new Rollerblade® in-line skates, too," said Barbie.

"That will be so much fun!" Christie answered, turning on the hand-held vacuum. "I bet the whole gang will want to go."

"We'll have a great time," said Barbie.

Just then, Ken and Alan walked in. They'd driven to town to pick up lunch. "Break time!" Alan called.

"Hey, this place looks super!" said Ken. "But the paint smell is still strong. Let's eat outside."

Kira and Steve joined them on the porch. So did Amy. The rainy weather had given way to glorious sunshine. Midge raised her cup of soda. "I want to toast Barbie," she said. "I'd have run out of here if it wasn't for her."

Barbie smiled happily. "It was my pleasure."

Ken hugged her. "Barbie, what would we do without you?"